# Tamlane

## RETOLD BY JUDY PATERSON

## ILLUSTRATED BY SALLY J. COLLINS

THE AMAISING PUBLISHING HOUSE LTD

## DEDICATION
For Jennie
who loves a little white horse

## NOTES

This traditonal ballad from the 13th century is sometimes known as Tam Lin. It is set in the Etterick Valley, on lands of the Earl of Dunbar and March, where indeed lived Thomas the Rhymer. The fairies liked to steal small children, preferably babies who had not been christened, to bring them up as their own. Woods and wells were magical places, maybe a warning to small children to stay close to home.

I chose to use the spelling *Tamlane* as used in a 19th century collection of ballads. Here are the parting words of the Fairy Queen.

> "Had I but kenn'd Tamlane," she says,
> Before ye cam frae hame,
> I wad ta'en out your heart o' flesh,
> Put in a heart o stane."

## GLOSSARY
WORDS IN ORDER AS THEY APPEAR IN TEXT

| | |
|---|---|
| *bonny* | pretty |
| *mantle* | cloak |
| *laird* | a noble lord |

Text © Judy Paterson
Illustrations © Sally J. Collins

Published in 1999 by
**The Amaising Publishing House Ltd.** Unit 7, Greendykes Industrial Estate,
Broxburn, West Lothian, EH52 6PG, Scotland

*Telephone:* 01506-857570
*Fax:* 01506-858100
*E-mail:* Amaising.bx@btinternet.com
*URL:* http://www.btinternet.com/~amaising.com

ISBN 1 871512 62 X

Printed and bound by Scotprint Ltd, Musselburgh

Page layout by Mark Blackadder

Reprint Code 10 9 8 7 6 5 4 3 2 1

In Ettrickdale, many long years ago, Randolph, Earl of Murray had a fine young son named Tamlane.

Dunbar, Earl of March, had a bonny daughter called Janet and, since the two children lived nearby, they often played together.

Then one day, when Tamlane was nine years old he disappeared.

"Where is he?" little Janet wanted to know.

"I wish we knew," sighed Tamlane's worried father. "We've hunted high and low, but there's no sign of him or his white horse."

"He went riding through the forest of Carterhaugh to visit his uncle," whispered the serving maid. "He's been taken by the fairy folk."

"Will they keep him?" Janet asked. "Can I still go and play with him?"

"Oh no!" exclaimed the old nurse in fright. "You just stay away from Carterhaugh. You just stay away from wells and woods altogether or you'll be taken by the fairy folk too!"

# A

nd so the years passed and Tamlane's playmates grew up. Sometimes they wondered about Tamlane.

"The fairies changed him into a strange beast," some said.

"If you go deep into the woods and find the fairy well," others whispered to each other, "Tamlane will cast a spell upon you."

Some thought it was nonsense, but others thought it was true.

"I shall find out for myself," thought Janet who had a brave heart.

One fine Spring day, Janet got up as the larks were singing high above the green fields. She put on her rose coloured gown, brushed her golden hair and held it back with a gold band. Then she took her green mantle and set off from her father's Hall just as the servants began the day's chores.

As Janet crossed the fields she startled the young rabbits and in the distance a fox watched her warily. She reached the forest without seeing anyone from the Great Hall or the nearby farm.

Janet wandered deeper and deeper into the forest. It grew more and more still and silent but she was not afraid

Then she came to a small clearing. Here the sunlight struggled through the dark trees. A white horse grazed quietly beside a well.

Janet stroked the horse and looked all around.

"Do you belong to Tamlane?" she asked, and she would not have been surprised if the horse had replied. Instead there was silence.

"I shall sit by the well and wait all day," said Janet quite loudly. "So if you are here Tamlane, come out and speak to me." She found a seat below the overhanging rosebush and made herself comfortable but Tamlane did not appear.

"I don't believe in fairies," she thought to herself as she picked a white rose.

Immediately a young man appeared before her. He was tall and handsome. His eyes were grey and he wore his long dark hair loose over his shoulders. Janet knew it was Tamlane.

"Why have you come to the woods, My Lady, and who gave you permission to pick roses from my well?" he asked.

Janet was not afraid and she replied with a bright smile,

"These woods are on the Carterhaugh Estate and since I am the Laird's daughter I may come and go as I please. I do not need your permission, Tamlane"

Tamlane laughed softly,

"These woods belong to the fairy folk brave lassie, and it is my job to protect it for them. You should be safe at home, wee Janet."

"So you do remember me!" said Janet. "But I'm not so wee any more Tamlane!" she said crossly. Then she frowned and looked worried. "Are you really one of the fairy folk?" she asked.

"I am one of the fairy folk, Janet," Tamlane replied as a shadow crossed his grey eyes. "But you remember that I was not always one of them."

Before Janet could think of anything to say, he held out his hand to her,

"Come with me Janet, and I will show you the fairy forest."

They spent a long time exploring the forest of Carterhaugh. It was a new and secret world for Janet who had never been there before. In the half light they looked for flowers and watched the squirrels at play.

When she noticed that daylight was fading Janet sighed,

"It is time I went home. I have been gone for such a long time. My father will be looking for me."

Tamlane smiled at her, "You have not been away for long. Do not fear."

J anet found her way home quickly. She slipped into the Hall without anyone seeing her. She hung up her mantle and brushed the leaves from the edge of her gown.

The servants came and went, still about their early morning chores, just as they had been when she left. The dog remained quiet by the hearth and her cat was still curled up on the window seat.

All was just as she had left it. No-one seemed to notice that she had even been away.

Summer came and each time Janet walked in the rose garden with her friends, she thought of Tamlane. When they were small, they had played hide and seek in the rose garden. Tamlane was always the last one to be found.

Janet listened carefully to anyone who told stories about the elves and fairies of the Border Country. She wondered if Tamlane was happy with the fairies or if he really wanted to come home again.

Soon it was autumn and the leaves were turning to gold and red. Janet looked across the fields to the silent, mysterious forest. She sighed when she thought of Tamlane's grey eyes and wondered if he missed his family as much as they missed him.

Janet loved Tamlane and she decided to see him again.

The day was crisp and snow was not far away. Janet wore her gown of peach and a hooded cloak as red as ripe cherry. She made her way to the well and found Tamlane's white horse was there just as before. But there was no sign of Tamlane.

The last white roses were still fragrant on the rosebush however, and Janet picked one. Instantly Tamlane stood before her.

"Why have you returned Janet?" he asked her.

"Tamlane, please tell me what you are. Are you a mortal man or are you one of the fairy folk?"

"I am still a mortal man but I am under the spell of the Queen of Fairies," he replied.

"Would you like to be with your family again?" Janet asked him.

"Indeed I would!" sighed Tamlane.

"Then forget these fairies. Come home now," Janet encouraged him.

"How I wish I could! However, because of the spell I cannot leave this forest, Janet. This queen is not one of the good fairies. Every seven years she pays her due to the devil with a mortal man and I fear I may be the next mortal man," he said looking sad and troubled.

Janet felt frightened. She pointed to the white horse, "Take your horse and come with me. My father will protect you," she said jumping up and reaching out to take his hand.

"There is only one way to save me Janet,"
said Tamlane. "If you love me, then tonight, Hallowe'en, is
the one night in the year you can break the spell which holds me."

"What must I do?" asked Janet.

"At midnight the fairy folk will ride out to Miles Cross by the town. The
Queen will be on her great black stallion, then the King of Elves will ride a
fine brown horse. I will be riding my milk-white steed." Tamlane stroked the
gentle horse. "You must pull me down from the horse and hold me in your
arms no matter what happens. The Fairy Queen will change me into all
kinds of beasts. Hold me fast. When you feel I am a burning lead weight, do
not let go. Carry me to the water trough and throw me into the cool water.
Then wrap me in your green mantle and your love will have saved me."

"I will save you," promised Janet as she turned for home. "I shall be at
Miles Cross at midnight."

There was a new moon that Hallowe'en. Janet wrapped herself in her warm green mantle and walked to Miles Cross at the edge of the town. An owl hooted softly and a fox stepped across her path. The north wind carried strange sounds and Janet shivered.

At midnight exactly she saw a shimmer of light from fairy lanterns and she heard the jingle of tiny bells. The procession passed her. First came the Queen on her prancing black stallion and then came the King of Elves on his proud brown horse. The third horse was milk-white and Janet wasted not a moment. She jumped up and dragged Tamlane from the saddle. They tumbled onto the ground and she clung to him for dear life.

All around, the fairies ran screeching and screaming.

Janet held on to Tamlane and then there was a blinding blue flash. She was suddenly holding a clammy, cold, silvery snake. It wriggled and coiled itself about her arms. For a moment she was so frightened, Janet tried to free herself.

Then she reminded herself it was Tamlane. Janet shut her eyes, remembered how much she loved Tamlane, and she clung to the snake for dear life.

Suddenly the scales turned to fur beneath her fingers and a great growling sound deafened her. Janet clung to the arm of the large hairy beast and found herself lifted into the air by an enormous bear.

Her heart beat so fast and she was so frightened she nearly let go. Then she remembered how much she loved Tamlane, and clung to the great bear for dear life.

Then a foul smelling, hot breath hit her face and she nearly fainted. She fell to the ground but her fingers were tangled deep into the shaggy mane of a yellow-eyed lion. Janet closed her eyes as it roared above her and she thought she could not hang on to such a dreadful beast. Then she remembered how much she loved Tamlane and clung to the lion for dear life.

Finally Janet screamed out in pain. Her arms were full of a burning lead weight and she could not move. The Queen of Fairies stood over her and laughed while all around the screeching, screaming fairy folk ran faster and faster.

Janet felt her arms burning and thought of the cool waters of the well. Then she remembered what Tamlane had told her.

She struggled and limped until she reached the side of the ancient stone water trough. The fairy folk were suddenly still. Janet remembered Tamlane and clung to the burning lead weight for dear life. She lifted it up and threw it into the trough.

"I love you Tamlane," she cried.

The burning lead weight hissed in the water.

O ut of the hissing water stepped Tamlane. The Fairy Queen stood as stiff and cold as stone as she watched. Janet quickly wrapped her green mantle round his shoulders. Tamlane was safe.

"I would curse you if I could young lady, but your love keeps you safe." The Fairy Queen glared at Janet, "You have stolen my bonniest knight, my favourite groom. Tamlane is yours forever."

Janet shivered and Tamlane wrapped his arm around her shoulders,

"You are a bold, brave lassie Janet!" he said. "I am yours forever after."

"Just so long as you stay the way you are right now!" she laughed. "I never want to hug another snake, or bear, or lion, Tamlane."

Tamlane's horse whinnied softly as the first rays of sunlight crept over the hills. Two fox cubs chased each other through the bracken and birds began to greet the new day.

"Let's go home Janet," laughed Tamlane. "Your family will think you have been stolen by the fairies."

Indeed everyone was out searching for Janet.

"Look who I found," called Janet happily when she saw her old nurse.

The old woman took no notice and wagged her finger at Janet,

"I thought I told you to stay away from wells and woods, young lady. Why there's fairies and all manner of beasties in the woods."

"I know," laughed Janet. "I brought one home!"

The old nurse peered up at the tall young man and a great smile spread slowly over her wrinkled face.

"I can't believe it!" she gasped, "back from the fairies! You found Tamlane!"